Peppa Pig

and the
Family Reunion

This book is based on the TV series *Peppa Pig*.
Peppa Pig is created by Neville Astley and Mark Baker.
Peppa Pig © Astley Baker Davies Ltd/Entertainment One UK Ltd 2003.
www.peppapig.com

First edition 2019

Library of Congress Catalog Card Number pending
ISBN 978-1-5362-0615-9

18 19 20 21 22 23 APS 10 9 8 7 6 5 4 3 2 1

Printed in Humen, Dongguan, China

This book was typeset in Peppa.
The illustrations were created digitally.

Candlewick Entertainment
an imprint of Candlewick Press
99 Dover Street
Somerville, Massachusetts 02144

visit us at www.candlewick.com

Peppa Pig

and the

Family
Reunion

CANDLEWICK
ENTERTAINMENT

Peppa and George are very excited.

Today the Pig family is having a reunion!

Everyone in the family will be there.

Grandpa Pig and Granny Pig arrive first.

"You've brought pie!" says Peppa. "I love pie!"

"Mmmm," says George.

Here are Auntie Pig and Uncle Pig with Cousin Chloe and Baby Alexander.

Cousin Chloe is a big girl — bigger than Peppa.

Baby Alexander is very small.

Uncle Pig and Auntie Pig
unpack the car.
They have brought a lot
of stuff for the baby.

Daddy Pig helps Uncle Pig
unload a high chair,
some baby toys,
a stroller, and
even a bathtub!

Peppa likes Baby Alexander.

"Would you like to help feed the baby?" asks Auntie Pig.

"Oh, yes," says Peppa. She tries to feed Baby Alexander. He turns away.
Peppa tries again. The baby won't open his mouth.

"Try playing airplane," says Auntie Pig. She shows Peppa how to
fly the spoon into Baby Alexander's mouth. It works!

"Can you say airplane?" asks Peppa.

Baby Alexander can't talk yet.

Peppa wants to teach Baby Alexander to talk.
"Can you say dinosaur?"

"**Gah-gah,**" says Baby Alexander.

Later that night, it's time to put Baby Alexander to bed.

"No, what's that other noise?"

"That's the vacuum cleaner," says Chloe.

"Why are you vacuuming at night?" asks Daddy Pig.

"And why is Auntie Pig playing a trumpet?"

"Loud noises are the best way to get Baby Alexander to sleep!" shouts Uncle Pig. "We are a very noisy family!"

It is a very noisy night.

After breakfast the next morning,
everyone goes for a walk.
Peppa tries to teach Baby Alexander a new word.

"Look! A bird!" says Peppa.

"Goo-goo,"
says Baby Alexander.

"Sky!" says Peppa.

"Gaa-gaa," says Baby Alexander.

Then it's time for the family reunion lunch. They are having Peppa's favorite — spaghetti!

Daddy Pig and Uncle Pig love spaghetti, too.

Both of them ask for more.

For dessert, everyone has a piece of Granny Pig's pie.

"Yum!" Peppa says to Baby Alexander.

"Goo-goo!" says Baby Alexander.

Chloe has brought her puppet theater,
and she and Peppa and George
put on a puppet show.

They make a
Chloe puppet,

a Peppa
puppet,

and a dinosaur puppet
for George.

Everyone claps after the puppet show.
Well, almost everyone.
Daddy Pig and Uncle Pig have fallen asleep.

Peppa and Chloe
go outside to play before
the reunion is over.
Baby Alexander
likes to watch them
play in the mud.

"Look, Baby Alexander!"
says Peppa.
"We're jumping up
and down
in muddy puddles!"

And then it happens.

Baby Alexander says his first word:

"Puddles!"

Well done, Peppa!

Well done, Baby Alexander!